MARY HOFFMAN • JACKIE MORRIS
ANIMALS
• OF THE BIBLE •

FRANCES LINCOLN

CONTENTS

For Georgie Dell – M.H.

For Sophie and Mattie – J.M.

Animals of the Bible copyright © Frances Lincoln Limited 2002
Text copyright © Mary Hoffman 2002
Illustrations copyright © Jackie Morris 2002

First published in Great Britain in 2002 by
Frances Lincoln Limited, 4 Torriano Mews
Torriano Avenue, London NW5 2RZ

www.franceslincoln.com

British Library Cataloguing in Publication Data
available on request

ISBN 0-7112-1886-2

Set in Meridien Roman

Printed in Singapore

1 3 5 7 9 8 6 4 2

INTRODUCTION

*Have you ever heard the expression "a wolf in sheep's clothing"?
It means a bad person pretending to be kind and gentle and it comes
from the Bible. There are many sayings and stories in the Bible about
animals, perhaps because animals were an important part of people's
lives when the Old Testament was written.*

*The Holy Land was full of sheep and goats and camels and even,
in those days, lions. In the Book of Isaiah it says, "The wolf shall live
with the lamb, the leopard shall lie down with the kid, the calf and
the lion ... together, and a little child shall lead them."*

*For this book I have chosen some of the best-known Old Testament
stories which feature animals, from the first ones in the world to the
great whale that swallowed Jonah. All of them were doing God's will.*

I hope you will enjoy reading about them.

Mary Hoffman

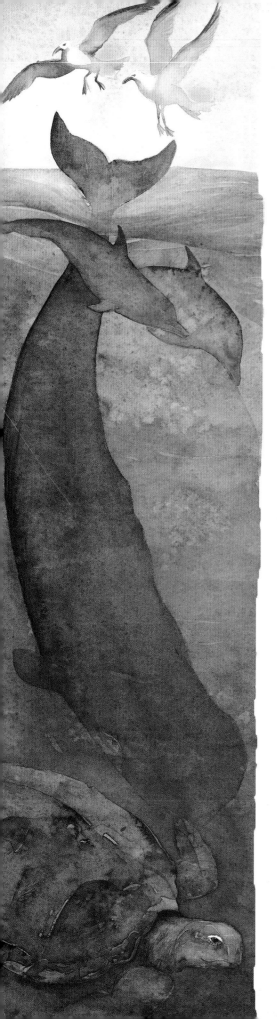

NAMING
the ANIMALS

God made the world in six days. First He made heaven and earth and the sun, moon and stars. On the fifth day He made all the birds of the air and all the fishes of the sea and the whales and dolphins too. On the sixth day He made all the creatures that crawl or slither on the ground, or walk on four legs or two, finishing with Adam and Eve, the first two humans.

Adam and Eve lived in the garden of Eden and God gave all the animals into their care. And then Adam had to invent names for all the creatures God had made. Can you imagine what an important job that was?

Imagine seeing for the first time a tiger, a kangaroo, a crocodile and a toucan and having to come up with the right names for them. And what about the potto, the wombat and the fat-tailed skink? You can see Adam was kept busy for a long time. Do you think he made good choices?

The SERPENT in the GARDEN

There was one animal in the garden that meant trouble for Adam and Eve. It was a slithery, slippery, great green snake. It was listening when God said to Adam and Eve, "You can eat everything you find growing in Eden except for the fruit of that big tree in the middle."

"You know why God doesn't want you to eat that fruit on the big tree," the snake hissed in Eve's ear. "He doesn't want you to be as powerful as Him."

Eve took no notice for a while. She had bananas and pineapples and apricots and mangoes and cherries and kumquats and many other tasty fruits to eat, so she didn't really mind not having any from the big tree in the middle of the garden.

But one day she fancied something different and saw that the forbidden fruit looked tempting. She picked one and took a big bite. It was delicious. She held it out to Adam and he ate some too.

When God found out what had happened, He wasn't just angry (although He was very angry indeed). He was sad too, because He had trusted Adam and Eve. "You shall crawl on your belly and eat dust all the days of your life!" He told the serpent.

But for Adam and Eve there was worse to come. God banished them from the beautiful garden of Eden and put a flaming sword in front of the gate so that they could never return. And that was the beginning of people's troubles on this earth.

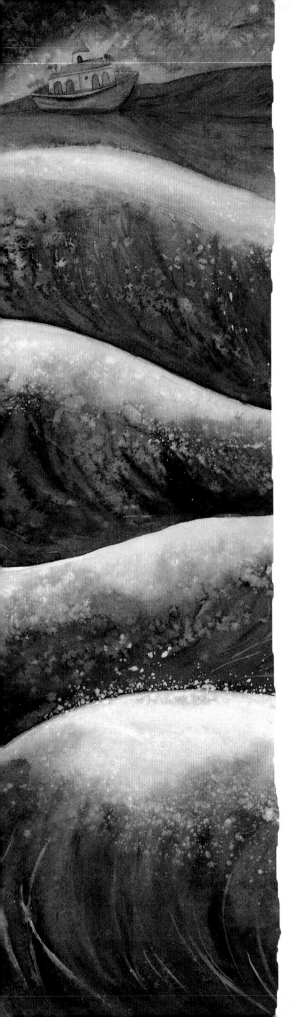

NOAH'S ARK

Many, many years after Adam and Eve left the garden of Eden, there was a good man called Noah. He had a wife and three sons, called Ham, Shem and Japheth. All the other people in the world, apart from this family, had forgotten all about God and become wicked. They were greedy and selfish and unkind to one another. God grew so angry with them that He decided to send a great flood and wash the world clean and start again.

But He told Noah what He was going to do and gave him instructions to build a huge wooden boat, an ark, which would float on the flood waters. God told Noah to collect two of every animal that walked, crawled, crept or flew and bring them aboard the ark.

So when the rain started, Noah's ark full of animals floated and he and his family and just two of every animal were saved from the flood. It was quite a squash inside the ark. The big animals sometimes sat on the little ones by mistake and the ones who had horns kept poking the ones who didn't.

When the rain stopped after forty days, Noah sent out a dove. It flew over the water but found no dry land and came back. Later, Noah sent the dove out again and it came back with a twig of green leaves in its beak. The third time Noah sent it out, the dove didn't come back at all.

So Noah knew the waters had gone down and he let the animals out of the ark. They came racing, flapping, leaping and creeping out of the ark and went off to find fresh food. They had cubs and kittens and calves and puppies and some of them had eggs – so all the animals of the world were saved. And Noah's sons and their wives had babies who grew up and had babies and so on, until all the people of the world were born – which makes us all part of the same family.

JACOB'S SHEEP

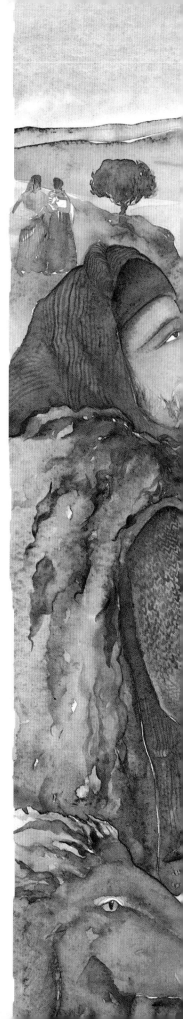

One of the descendants of Shem was Abraham, who had a son called Isaac. Isaac had two sons and the younger one, called Jacob, travelled a long way from home to work for a man named Laban.

Now this Laban was a cunning man and rather mean. He never paid Jacob any proper wages and when Jacob fell in love with Laban's daughter Rachel, he tricked him into marrying his older daughter Leah instead.

Well, in the end, Jacob married Rachel too and had children by both his wives. By then he'd had enough of working hard for Laban, looking after his sheep and cows and goats and never getting any proper wages. Besides, he had a large family to feed.

So he went to his father-in-law and said, "The time has come for me to go home with my wives and children and visit the land of my father, Isaac. What will you give me in return for all the work I have done for you these twenty years and more?"

Laban hated to part with anything that was his, so in the end Jacob said, "I'll tell you what. Let me take all the spotted and speckled cattle and sheep and goats and you can keep the rest," and Laban agreed. He didn't think there would be all that many spotted and speckled animals.

But Jacob knew far more about livestock than Laban did. He had been mating the strongest speckled and spotted animals together, so that he left with an enormous number of cows and sheep and goats and they were all the best ones! And Laban just had to put up with it.

And to this day you can see the lovely splotchy brown and white animals which are still known as "Jacob's Sheep".

 # PHARAOH'S DREAM

In the days of Jacob, the kings of Egypt were called "Pharaohs" and were very powerful. Jacob had twelve sons and his favourite one, Joseph, ended up in Egypt working for the Pharaoh.

This story is about a dream that the Pharaoh had. He heard that Joseph was good at explaining the meaning of dreams, so he called him to his royal palace and told him what he had seen in his sleep.

"There were seven fat cows grazing by a river," said the Pharaoh. "Their coats were glossy, their noses wet and their eyes clear and healthy. Then up out of the river came seven other cows – the stringiest, skinniest cattle I have ever seen. And – miraculous to see – these seven skeletons of cows ATE the seven fat ones and gobbled them all up! But the thin cows were

just as thin after their strange meal as before. What on earth can it mean?"

Joseph said, "It's not just a dream but a prophecy. Egypt will have seven good years when crops are plentiful and everyone has enough to eat, but then there will follow seven years of famine and your people will starve if you don't do anything about it. If you want my advice, you should keep something back from each harvest over the next seven years, so that when the hard times come, your people will have enough to eat."

It all happened as Joseph said it would and Pharaoh took all his advice. The person who handed out the food in the years when there wasn't much to go round, was Joseph himself. And from then on he became an important man in Egypt.

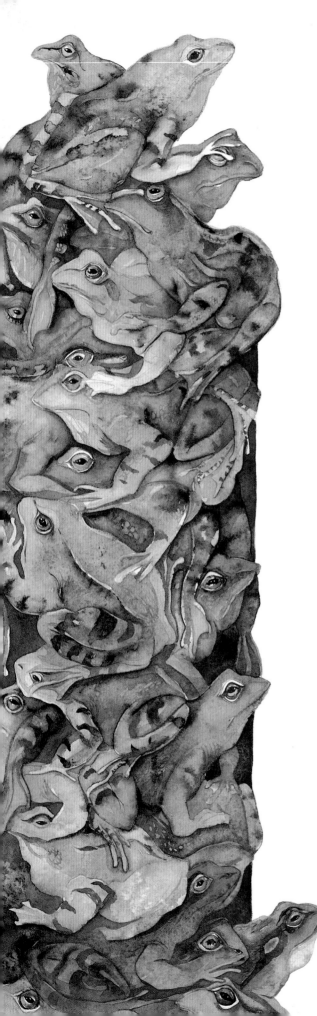

FROGS and CREEPY CRAWLIES

In the years that followed, the descendants of Joseph, who were called Israelites, were not treated well in Egypt. They became slaves to the Egyptians.

A great leader called Moses grew up among the Israelites. Moses asked the Pharaoh to let him take his people away from Egypt, but the Pharaoh said no.

How he came to regret it! Moses was a powerful man, who was close to God and he got Him to bring down ten plagues on Egypt.

There was a terrible plague of frogs. First they filled all the ponds and rivers and streams and then they hopped out on to the land and got into people's houses.

No-one could get into bed without finding it full of frogs. There were frogs in the food dishes and frogs in the ovens. Frogs on the stairs and frogs on the roof. Everyone was very miserable, except the frogs. The Pharaoh said he'd do anything Moses wanted if he would only get rid of the frogs. So Moses did. But the Pharaoh went back on his word and he still wouldn't let the Israelites go.

So the Egyptians suffered more plagues. First a terrible itching in their hair and then in their underclothes. This plague was of lice and soon everyone in Egypt was scratching and complaining, even the Pharaoh.

"All right, Moses," said Pharaoh. You can take your people. Just get rid of these lice!"

But as soon as the lice were gone, he broke his promise. So God sent a plague of flies and that was even worse. Flies on the food, flies in the drinking water, every stick of furniture or scrap of floor space black with buzzing, crawling, stinking flies.

You can guess what happened next. And after that God sent another plague – of locusts. They came like a thundercloud. The skies were filled with the rustle of their wings and the scraping sound of their back legs rubbing together. All Egypt was full of the sound.

Soon every ear of wheat was stripped to the stalk and there was nothing left for the Egyptians to eat.

Well, that Pharaoh never did keep his promise to Moses even when worse plagues came. But in the end Moses did lead his people out of slavery.

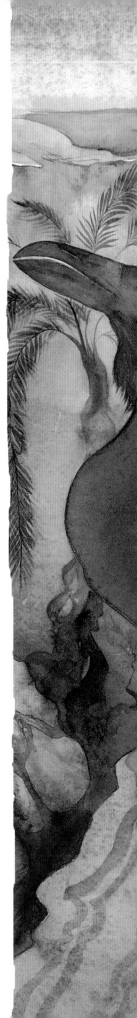

ELIJAH'S RAVENS

Many generations after the Israelites found their promised land, a new prophet came, called Elijah.

At that time, the Israelites seemed to have forgotten their true God, who helped them out of Egypt.

All except Elijah the prophet.

One day he heard God's voice. "You must leave your home, Elijah," He said, "and go and live in the wilderness beside the brook, Kerith."

"But how shall I live?" Elijah asked God. "There is nothing to eat or drink in the wilderness."

"You can drink water from the brook, and as for food, I shall send ravens to bring you bread and meat."

And that was how Elijah lived for a long time, drinking from the clear water of the brook, with the ravens bringing him food twice a day. Elijah performed many miracles after that and turned the Israelites' hearts back towards God.

DANIEL
in the LIONS' DEN

The troubles of God's chosen people, the Israelites, were far from over. The Babylonians captured Jerusalem, their holy city, and the Israelites became slaves again. One of the best-known and respected Israelites was a man called Daniel. The king, Darius, valued Daniel very highly and made him the chief prince of the kingdom.

This made the other princes jealous and they plotted to get rid of Daniel in the cruellest way. They went to King Darius and said, "There should be a law that no-one must pray to any god or man except you, great king. If you hear of any man praying to a god, he should be thrown to the lions."

Reluctantly the king, who was a kind man, agreed. Now Daniel was a very good man, who prayed to God three times a day and he didn't change his ways when the new law came into force. It wasn't long before the jealous princes saw him praying at his window. They dragged him before the king.

Darius was very unhappy about it, but he had made the law, so he agreed that Daniel must be thrown into a cave full of lions. A stone was rolled in front of the cave mouth and sealed with the king's own ring.

Then Darius spent a sleepless night worrying about his friend Daniel. But he needn't have worried, for God sent an angel to the cave, who held the lions' mouths shut. And when King Darius came trembling to the cave the next morning, he found Daniel alive and well and still singing God's praises. The king was so impressed that he ordered all his people to change to Daniel's religion – and they did.

And as for the princes who had accused Daniel, they became the lions' dinner instead of him.

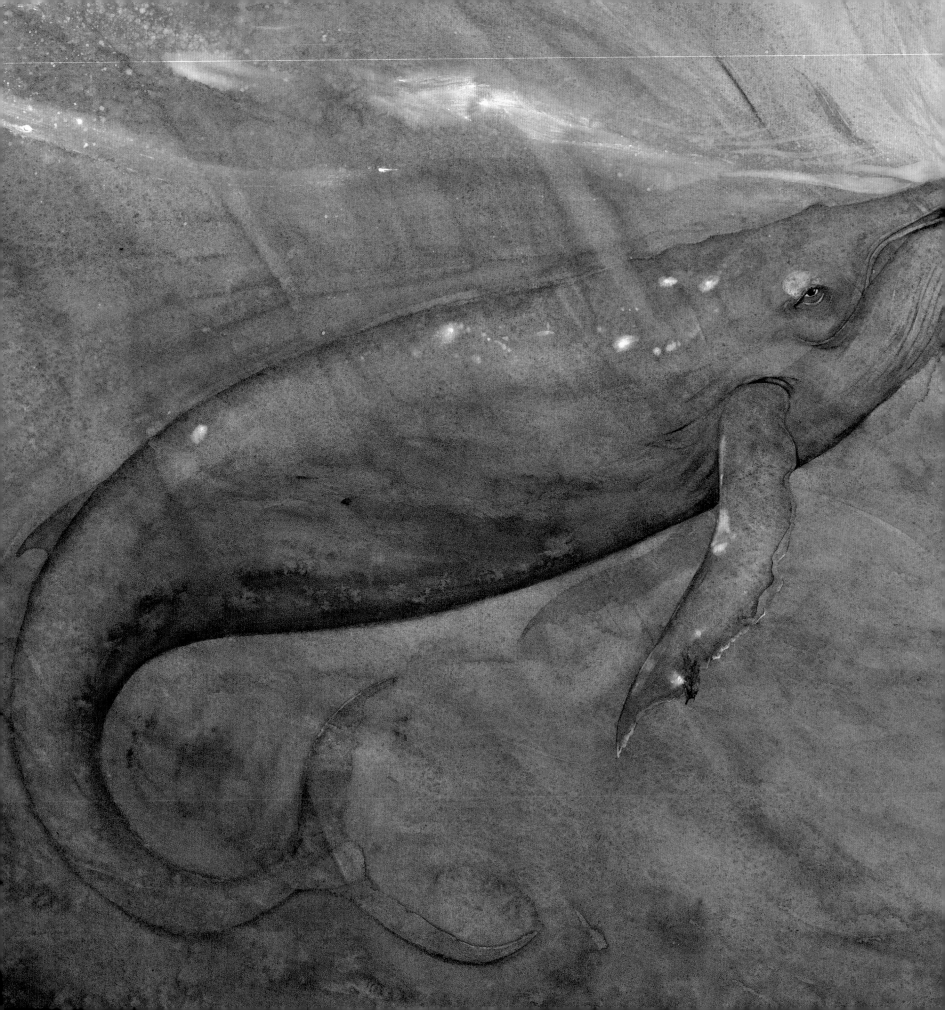

JONAH
and the WHALE

There is a story in the Bible that shows how hard it is to resist God's wishes when He wants you to do something. God was angry with the people of Nineveh, who had turned their backs on Him and become very wicked. He came to a man called Jonah and told him to go to the city of Nineveh and remind them about God.

Jonah didn't want to say no to God, but he didn't want to go, so he crept aboard a ship that was sailing in the opposite direction. But it is difficult to avoid God when He has a job in mind for someone. A great storm blew up and Jonah was thrown overboard by the sailors, who realised that he must have offended God in some way.

Just imagine how miserable Jonah was as he sank through the waves! He was sure he was going to drown. But a big mouth came scooping through the water and swallowed him up. It belonged to a whale which God had sent and Jonah spent three days and nights in its belly. All the time he was inside, he prayed to God for forgiveness.

The whale was swimming strongly. On the fourth day, it arrived at the coast and threw up Jonah on to the shore. (It must have been glad to get rid of the indigestible prophet.)

"Now," said God, "will you go to Nineveh?"

And Jonah did. He told the people to stop being wicked or God would destroy them. And the people listened to him and were sorry for all the bad things they had done.

So God did not destroy them after all and then Jonah was angry with God! He was sitting under a shady tree outside the city and started to tell God off for sparing the people of Nineveh.

God made the sun shine so hard on Jonah's tree that it withered up and died and then Jonah had no shade at all.

"Are you sorry about the tree?" asked God.

"Yes," said Jonah.

"You did not plant it or water it," said God. "And yet you feel sorry for it. I made the people of Nineveh – don't you think I should feel sorry for them and spare them from destruction?"

And Jonah was silent, because he knew God was right.

ABOUT the STORIES

*If you want to read about any of these animals
in the Bible, this is where to look them up:*

NAMING THE ANIMALS
Genesis 2: 19-20
This is a conflation of two versions of creation given in Genesis.

THE SERPENT IN THE GARDEN
Genesis 3: 1-15

NOAH'S ARK
Genesis 6, 7, 8, 9: 1-17
I haven't included the rainbow and God's promise, because this book
is focusing on the animals.

JACOB'S SHEEP
Genesis 30: 25-40
I have left out the bit with the peeled willow-rods, which implies
sympathetic magic and would be very hard to explain.

PHARAOH'S DREAM
Genesis 41: 14-21; interpretation 25-43

FROGS AND CREEPY CRAWLIES
Exodus 8: 1-14, 15-19, 20-31; 10: 3-15

ELIJAH'S RAVENS
1 Kings 17: 1-7

DANIEL IN THE LIONS' DEN
Daniel 6: 4-23

JONAH AND THE WHALE
Jonah 1, 2, 3
Of course, the Bible says "a great fish", but it is traditional to make
it a whale, a sea-mammal, because it is hard to imagine a fish big
enough to swallow a man whole.

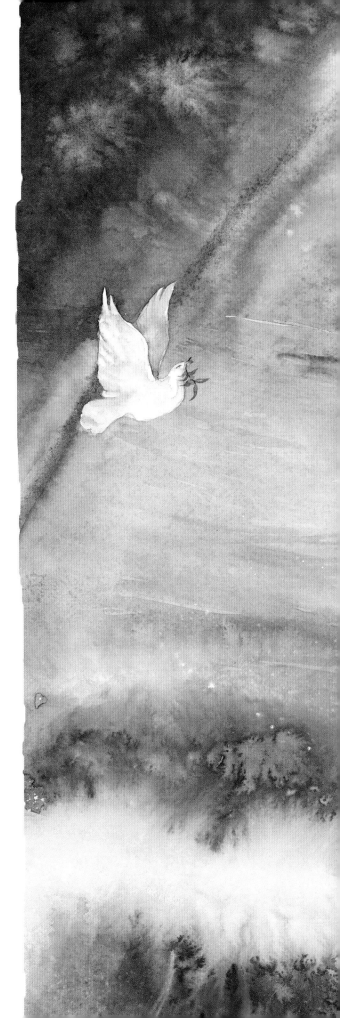